For Ned and Nina

For my parents, Audrey and Clint Heyd

FIRST SAIL

By Richard Henderson
Illustrated by Jennifer Heyd Wharton

Tidewater Publishers
Centreville, Maryland

Adam had never been to sea. His home was in an inland city; so, despite his strong interest in boats and the sea, Adam had not learned to sail. He was beginning to think he would never learn, when the letter came.

It was just an ordinary envelope, but it held an exciting invitation for Adam to spend the summer with his cousin Beth McNear. Beth was four years older than Adam, and her family lived on the bank of a large river that emptied into a great bay. Best of all, Beth had her own boat—a beautiful fifteen-foot sloop. Adam would have a chance to sail!

It was the day after he arrived at the McNears' that Beth broke the news.

"I've got a surprise for you, Adam," she said. "Mom has packed a lunch for us and we're off for a sail to Dutch Ship Island."

"Super!" shouted Adam. "Will you teach me to sail?"

"Well, probably not in one day," replied Beth, "but I can make a good start."

The two cousins left for the dock.

"Here it is!" said Beth proudly when they reached her little sloop. "I named it *Gull's Wing.*"

"Wow, it's neat!" Adam exclaimed.

Adam helped Beth slide the boat off the floating dock into the water. "This open place where we sit is called the *cockpit,*" said Beth. "You know, sailors have a language of their own, and the first thing for you to do is learn the right names for each part of the boat. For instance, the front is called the *bow* and the back is the *stern.*"

Beth sat down on the little cockpit seat and started to uncoil the mainsheet.

"Sailors call a rope a *line,*" she continued, "and the lines that pull a sail up are *halyards,* while the ones that pull a sail in are called *sheets.*"

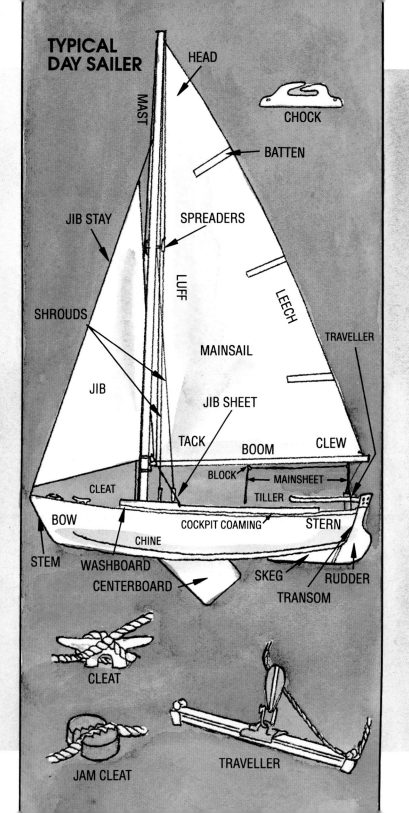

TYPICAL DAY SAILER

HEAD · CHOCK · BATTEN · MAST · JIB STAY · SPREADERS · LUFF · LEECH · SHROUDS · MAINSAIL · TRAVELLER · JIB · JIB SHEET · TACK · BOOM · CLEW · BLOCK · MAINSHEET · CLEAT · TILLER · BOW · COCKPIT COAMING · STERN · CHINE · STEM · WASHBOARD · CENTERBOARD · SKEG · RUDDER · TRANSOM

CLEAT

JAM CLEAT

TRAVELLER

3

SAIL FITTINGS

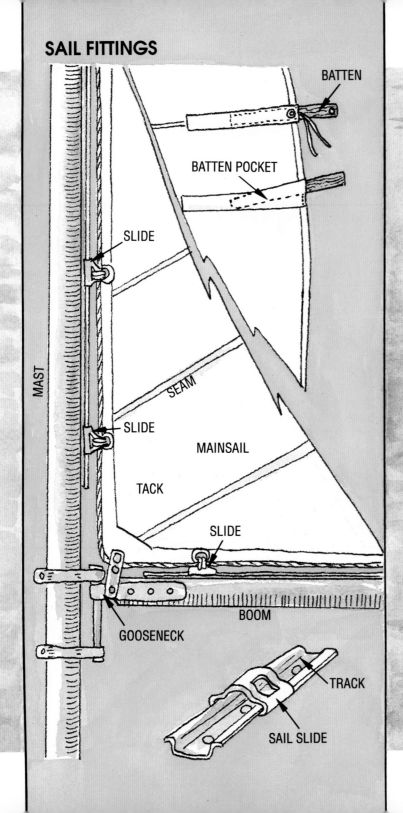

BATTEN

BATTEN POCKET

SLIDE

MAST

SEAM

SLIDE

MAINSAIL

TACK

SLIDE

GOOSENECK

BOOM

TRACK

SAIL SLIDE

4

"What's that for?" asked Adam, as he watched his cousin lean over the stern and hang the *rudder.*

"This is what makes the boat turn," Beth replied. "After I slip the *tiller* into the rudder head, I'll be able to steer the boat. The rudder turns on hinges called *gudgeons* and *pintles,* and the force of the water on one side of the rudder makes the boat turn. Just remember two things: you always push the tiller in the opposite direction from the one you want to turn, and the boat has to be moving through the water for the rudder to work."

Beth dumped the sails out of their bag and began to insert thin strips of wood called *battens* into pockets on the edge of each sail.

"Battens hold out a sail's *leech;* that's the back edge," she explained. "Now we're ready to put the mainsail on. We'll start with the *head,* which is the top of the sail. The two bottom corners are the *tack,* which attaches near the mast, and the *clew,* which attaches to the outhaul line on the other end of the boom."

"Some sails have little cars at the luff or front edge, and they slide on a mast track. But our mast has a long slot in its after side, so we just feed the luff's bolt rope into the slot as the sail is hoisted.

"The jib is a little different," Beth continued. "It hooks on the jib stay with small hanks that can slide up and down the stay as the jib is raised or lowered."

Then she lowered the *centerboard.* It was inside a narrow slot called the *centerboard well,* which was inside the centerboard trunk that stood upright in the middle of the cockpit. Beth explained that the board slid down into the water through a slot in the boat's bottom, and kept the boat from going sideways on certain points of sailing.

"Now all we have to do is hoist the sails and we can get under way," said Beth. "Watch out for the boom swinging back and forth," she warned as she pulled up the mainsail. "Don't let it hit your head!"

They were ready to go!

Beth cast off the bow line and gave the bow a good push away from the floating dock as she jumped back aboard.

"See how the boat comes to life when the wind strikes the sail?" she asked gleefully. She pulled the tiller toward her with one hand and pulled the mainsheet in with the other. "A boat is just like a living thing when it's under way."

"We're kind of leaning over, though," said Adam a little anxiously.

"Oh, that's normal," Beth reassured him. "It's the force of the wind against the sails that makes a boat heel over. Let me tell you something about the wind.

"Before you can learn to sail, you have to be able to tell which way the wind is blowing. Some boats have *wind indicators* on top of their masts that show the wind direction. I don't have one; instead, I use short ribbons called telltales tied to the shrouds. It's a good thing to learn how to determine wind direction by looking and feeling. On a day when the wind is fresh, you can feel it blowing on your face. If there's only a light breeze, you can lick your finger and hold it up in the air, and the side that feels cold will be the direction the breeze is blowing from."

"I've noticed something else," said Adam. "Those anchored boats are all pointing in the same direction."

"That's true," Beth agreed. "If they're anchored from the bow and there's no current, they always point into the wind. Another way to tell the direction of the wind is by watching which way the ripples are being blown across the top of the water."

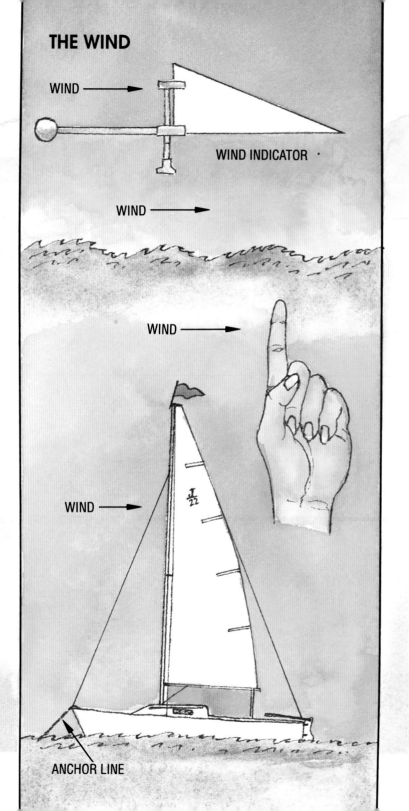

THE WIND

WIND

WIND INDICATOR

WIND

WIND

WIND

ANCHOR LINE

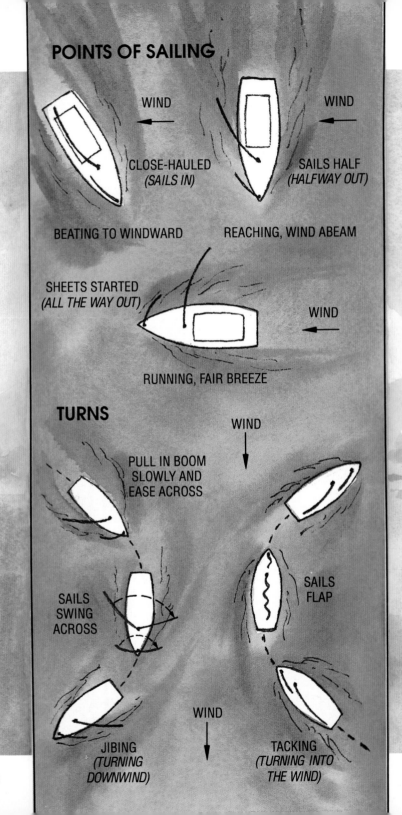

POINTS OF SAILING

WIND

WIND

CLOSE-HAULED
(SAILS IN)

SAILS HALF
(HALFWAY OUT)

BEATING TO WINDWARD

REACHING, WIND ABEAM

SHEETS STARTED
(ALL THE WAY OUT)

WIND

RUNNING, FAIR BREEZE

TURNS

WIND

PULL IN BOOM
SLOWLY AND
EASE ACROSS

SAILS
FLAP

SAILS
SWING
ACROSS

JIBING
(TURNING
DOWNWIND)

WIND

TACKING
(TURNING INTO
THE WIND)

As soon as the little boat was clear of the dock and the yachts at anchor, Beth began to show her cousin the *points of sailing*.

"Let's try to sail into the wind," she said while pulling in on the sheets.

"Now the sails just flap and we've stopped moving!" exclaimed Adam.

"That's right," Beth answered. "So we have to pull our sails all the way in and steer away from the wind—or *bear off,* as sailors say—until the sails stop flapping. Then we sail as far into the wind as possible without letting the sails flap. We call this *beating to windward.*"

"If we steer further away from the wind," she continued, "so that it blows on our side or *beam,* we are *reaching* and we let the sails out some, but not all the way.

"As for the last point," she concluded, "we let the mainsail out till the boom almost touches the *shroud* or side stay and turn the boat so that the wind is behind us, blowing on our stern. This is called *running.*"

After demonstrating the points of sailing, Beth showed Adam two ways of turning the boat completely around so that the sail and boom crossed over to the boat's other side. First, she turned into the wind so that the boom came over the middle of the boat and the sails flapped; then she let the boat continue to turn in that direction until the sails filled with wind on the other side. She explained that such a turn was called *tacking* or *coming about.*

Next, Beth made the little sloop run before the wind with the breeze directly behind, and she turned it so that the wind caught the sail from the other side and the boom suddenly swung across.

"That is called *jibing,*" she said, "and it is often used in moderate winds to rescue a person who has fallen overboard. Don't forget to duck your head."

"Well, that's your first lesson," said Beth. "Now I guess we had better be heading for Dutch Ship Island." She turned the sloop toward the river's main channel. The little boat raced downriver with a curling white wave at the bow and a frothy wake following at the stern.

"What's that?" shouted Adam as they passed a red metal structure with a gull sitting on top.

"A lighted gong buoy," answered Beth. "It marks the channel for big boats. There are all kinds of buoys and other channel markers," she added. "*Beacons, flashers, piles with dayboards, bells, whistles, nuns, cans, midchannel, junction* or *obstruction,* and even more. United States channel markers are mostly colored red or green. Midchannel buoys are red and white, while junction markers have bands of red and green with the color of the top band showing the preferred channel. Here's an easy rule to remember in following a marked channel. It's simple: *red, right, returning.* In other words, you keep the red buoys on your right going into a harbor, while doing just the opposite, keeping them on your left, coming out.

"Most buoys are numbered," Beth went on. "The green ones are odd and the red ones are even. Sometimes the color of a marker is hard to see from a distance, particularly if you're looking into the sun, so some buoys have a particular shape that tells you what they are. *Cans* are shaped like soda cans, and are usually green. Some red buoys look like upside-down ice-cream cones; they're called *nuns.*"

MARKERS AND BUOYS

NUN

CAN

JUNCTION OR OBSTRUCTION

MIDCHANNEL DAYMARK

LIGHTED MIDCHANNEL BUOY

SAFETY EQUIPMENT

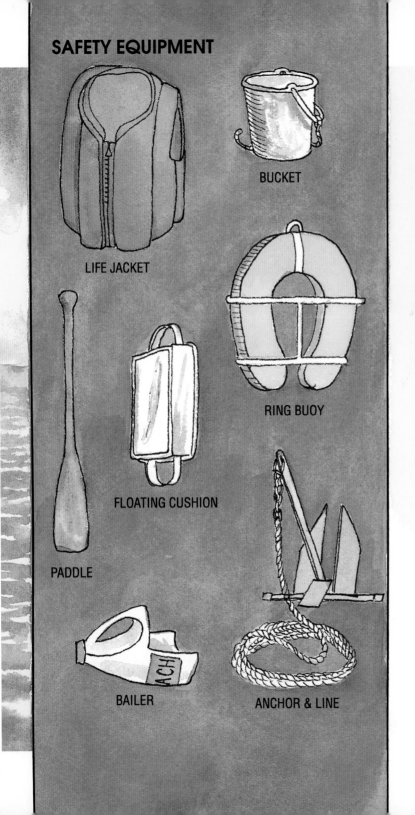

LIFE JACKET

BUCKET

PADDLE

FLOATING CUSHION

RING BUOY

BAILER

ANCHOR & LINE

In a short while *Gull's Wing* passed by the last buoy in the river and headed out into the bay. Beth's tone of voice became a little more serious.

"Before we get out into open waters," she said, "you should know something about water safety. Tell me, what safety equipment do you think a boat should carry?"

Adam thought for a moment. "Life jackets," he answered.

"Good!" said his cousin. There should be at least one life jacket, vest, or bib for each person on board and at least one throwable life preserver. What else do you think a boat like this should carry?"

"The only other things I can think of are an anchor, a horn, and a paddle," Adam replied after some hesitation.

"That's right," agreed Beth, "but don't forget the anchor line, and, of course, one of the most important items—a large bailer or bucket in case we shipped a lot of water or capsized. Speaking of capsizing, let me tell you a good rule to remember: *If your boat turns over, hang on to it.* Don't try to swim for shore even if you're a good swimmer. If your boat can be capsized by the wind, it will also float and keep you afloat.

"Here's another important rule I ought to tell you," Beth continued. "I've already mentioned it. If someone falls overboard from a small boat in moderate winds, first throw him a life preserver and then jibe around to pick him up. A jibe is quick and it puts you close to the person and in the best position to rescue him. Just before getting to him, slack your sails and head into the wind so the boat will slow down."

All of a sudden, Beth pointed up to windward. "Look, see that island over there?"

"Is that Dutch Ship Island?" Adam inquired eagerly.

"You got it," said Beth, "but it's directly upwind from us so we'll have to beat to windward in order to get there. We're on a *port tack* now because the wind is blowing from our *port* or left side, but in a little while we'll tack so that we'll be on a *starboard tack* with the wind on our *starboard* or right side. Then we'll tack again so that we make a sort of zigzag course toward the island. It's important to know which tack you're on because a sailboat on the starbord tack has the right of way over one on the port tack. In other words, the port tack boat has to keep clear."

"Is there anything I can do?" asked Adam.

"Sure," said Beth. "Your job will be to handle the jib sheets. When we tack, I'll say 'hard-a-lee,' and you can let loose the jib sheet. Then, after we tack, you can *trim the jib*; that means pull in the sheet on the other side and insert it in the jam cleat.

"There is quite an art in sailing a boat to windward," Beth explained to her cousin. "If you point the boat up into the wind too far, your sails will *luff* or begin to flap, and right away you'll feel the boat begin to slow down. Then, on the other hand, if you *bear off*, or sail too far away from the wind, your sails will be full and you'll be going fast but not making enough distance to windward. You have to be somewhere in between, and you can only really learn by practicing. One way to tell if you're beating properly is to see if your heading on one tack is at right angles or 90° to your heading on the other tack."

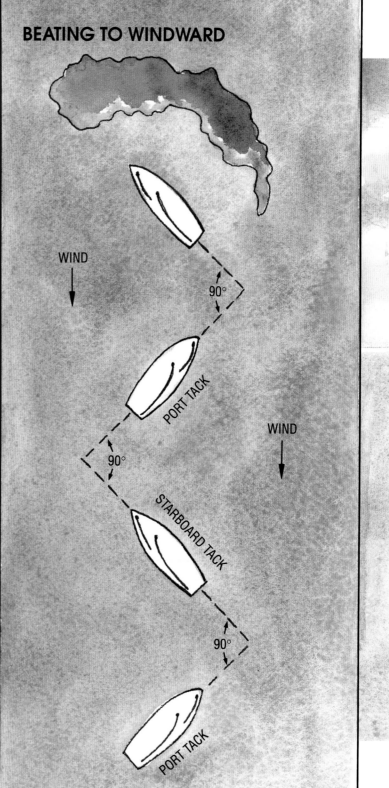

BEATING TO WINDWARD

WIND

90°

PORT TACK

WIND

90°

STARBOARD TACK

90°

PORT TACK

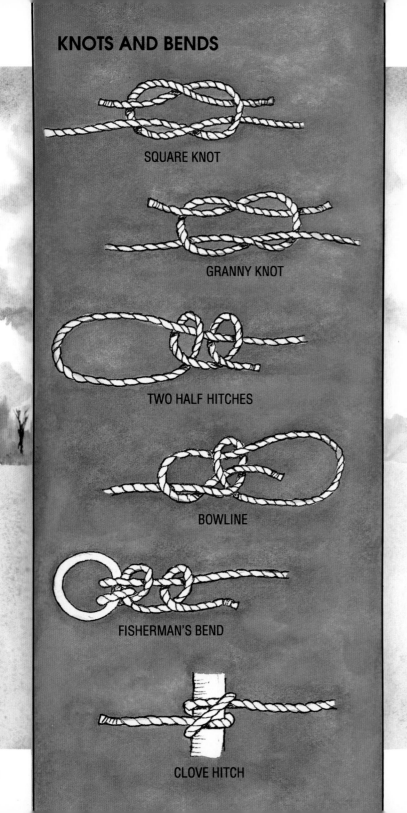

KNOTS AND BENDS

SQUARE KNOT

GRANNY KNOT

TWO HALF HITCHES

BOWLINE

FISHERMAN'S BEND

CLOVE HITCH

Soon the cousins were close to the shore of Dutch Ship Island. It was a beautiful, uninhabited island, covered by green woods. They could even smell the pine trees. A high clay bank curved along a white sandy beach, and at one end was a narrow point with long marsh grass growing over it.

Beth picked a smooth spot on the beach for a landing. Then, swinging the sloop around, she headed for shore on a broad reach. At the last minute before landing, she pulled up the centerboard so that the bow could run up on the dry sand before the boat ran aground.

After a gentle grounding, Beth and Adam lowered the sails, jumped ashore, and pulled *Gull's Wing* up as far as they could.

Beth took the bow line up to a big piece of driftwood and proceeded to make it fast.

"What kind of a knot is that?" asked Adam.

"It's called a *bowline*," Beth replied, as she showed him how to tie it. "This is the sailor's most useful knot because it won't slip and yet it will never jam." Then she showed Adam some other knots.

"The *square knot* is also very useful," she said, "but if the ends don't come through the loop together, it's a *granny knot*, and it will slip if it gets much strain. Some other useful knots are *two half hitches* and the *clove hitch* for tying onto a post or spar. Then, there's a *fisherman's bend*, which is used to tie a line onto an anchor ring or shackle."

When *Gull's Wing* was properly secured, the cousins set out to explore, pretending that they were shipwrecked on a desert island.

It didn't take long, however, to remember the lunch that Mrs. McNear had packed: sandwiches, potato chips, and sodas. There were even cookies for dessert.

"There sure are a lot of boats out sailing in the bay," Adam observed.

Beth's mouth was full of sandwich, so she couldn't speak, but she nodded in agreement.

"I see two yawls and a schooner," she finally said.

"What are yawls and schooners?"

"Well, they're sailboats with certain special rigs," Beth explained. "They each have two masts, but with a *yawl,* the big mast or *mainmast* is forward near the bow and the little mast, called a *mizzenmast,* is in the stern. A *schooner* has the mainmast nearer the stern and her smaller mast, or *foremast,* near the bow. A *ketch* is very much like a yawl, except that the mizzen is a little farther forward and a bit bigger than a yawl's."

Kicking away the loose pebbles and shells, Beth picked up a stick and began to draw diagrams of sailing rigs in the sand.

"Sloops, cutters and catboats only have one mast," she said. "The reason for their different names is the position of the mast. A catboat's mast is way up in the bow and there's no jib. With a *sloop* like *Gull's Wing,* the mast is about one-third of the boat's length from the bow. On a *cutter,* the mast is farther aft, almost in the center of the boat."

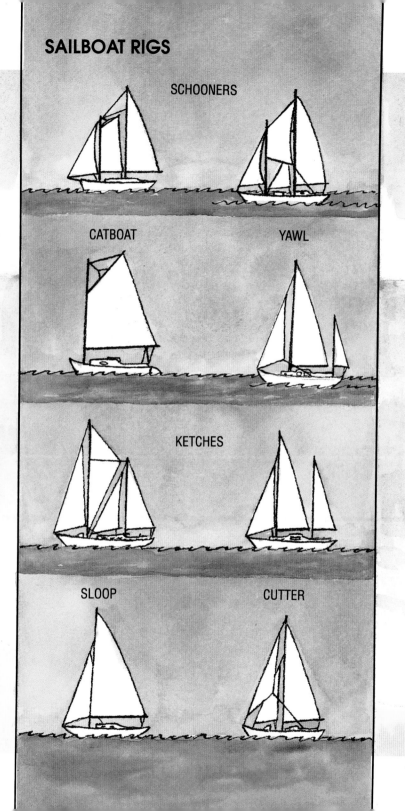

SAILBOAT RIGS

SCHOONERS

CATBOAT

YAWL

KETCHES

SLOOP

CUTTER

THEORY OF SAILING

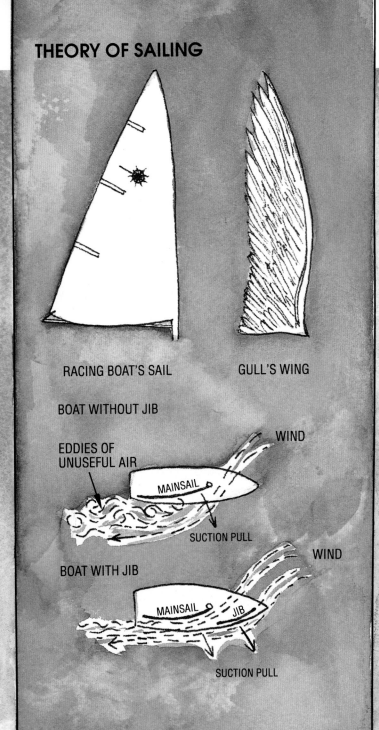

RACING BOAT'S SAIL

GULL'S WING

BOAT WITHOUT JIB

WIND

EDDIES OF UNUSEFUL AIR

MAINSAIL

SUCTION PULL

BOAT WITH JIB

WIND

MAINSAIL

JIB

SUCTION PULL

After lunch, the two cleaned up and Beth threw what scraps of food were left into the air for the sea gulls to snatch.

"We never throw stuff in the water," said Beth, "and it's against the law to throw anything overboard."

Soon the sky was full of screeching gulls—diving, wheeling, and flashing white in the sun as they fought over the scraps.

"The way they fly is awesome," Adam observed.

"It sure is," Beth agreed. "Did you know that their wings are almost like sails? I mean, sails and wings work sort of the same way. In fact, some masts and sails are purposely designed to be like birds' wings."

"But what does make them work?" asked Adam. "I can see that it's the push of the wind when a boat is running, but I can't understand how a boat can reach or beat to windward."

"Well, it's the flow of wind around a curved sail," Beth explained. "On the *leeward* or downwind side, a partial vacuum or sucking force is created which actually pulls the boat along. With a bird, this force is a lifting power.

"The jib forms a slot between itself and the mainsail which lets through a current of air along the lee side of the mainsail. This increases the suction pull partly by forcing more air around the lee side of the jib and helping to clear away harmful eddies or back swirls to leeward of the mainsail. I'll bet you didn't know that some birds actually have a tuft of feathers in front of each wing, and the tuft acts just like a jib."

Beth turned toward the west as her gaze followed the flight of a gull. Suddenly, she noticed a billowing dark cloud rising over the horizon.

"Uh-oh!" she exclaimed. "That's a thunderhead! We'd better get going."

"What's a thunderhead?" asked Adam, looking at the sky.

"It's a storm cloud, and if it forms to the west of us, we usually get a bad storm. Thunderheads often appear after a hot morning in the middle of summer."

"Do they look different from other clouds?" Adam asked.

"Yes," Beth replied. "There are all kinds of clouds, like the high thin wisps that sailors call *mare's tails*—a lot of those can predict wind. The lumpy, billowy clouds are called *cumulus* and usually mean good weather. And there are grey, low-flying, rain clouds called *scud*. But a *thunderhead* is a heavy mass of lumpy clouds that rises straight up like a tower. Sometimes the top fans out in wisps. The bottom is usually dark and ragged, and when it's close, you can often see rain or lightning."

"We'd better hurry, then!" exclaimed Adam, looking alarmed.

"Right!" agreed Beth. "Of course, if the cloud was closer, it would be safer to stay here, but I think we have plenty of time to get back before the storm hits."

Beth put on her life jacket, and the cousins quickly stowed their gear and pushed *Gull's Wing* out into the water. Beth grabbed the oar and paddled out until she could lower the centerboard. Then she headed into the wind so they could hoist the sails, and they were under way.

CLOUDS AND WEATHER

CIRRUS *(MARE'S TAIL)*

CUMULUS

CUMULONIMBUS *(THUNDERHEAD)*

SCUD

HEAVY WEATHER SAILING

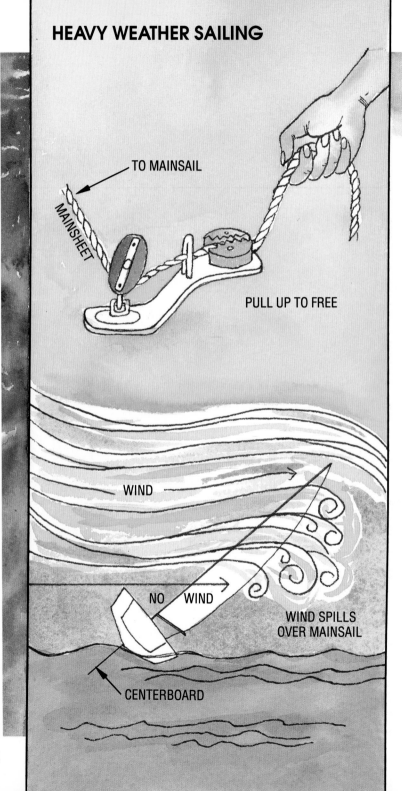

TO MAINSAIL

MAINSHEET

PULL UP TO FREE

WIND

NO WIND

WIND SPILLS
OVER MAINSAIL

CENTERBOARD

The wind had freshened and shifted around to the west, and when they sailed out from the shelter of the island, they felt its full force. The little sloop heeled over and the cousins quickly climbed up to the windward deck on the high side.

"Don't be scared," Beth said calmly. "Our weight up here will keep the boat from heeling over too far."

"Suppose we get a real strong puff?" asked Adam a little nervously.

"Well, there are two ways to keep from capsizing in a strong wind," said Beth. "One is to *luff up* when you begin to heel over too far. You push the tiller away from you, toward the lee side of the boat, so that the bow heads into the wind, making the sails luff. The other way to prevent tipping over is to let out your mainsheet. A good rule to remember is: *Never cleat the mainsheet in a small boat* unless there's a jam cleat that allows it to be freed with one quick pull. When there's a standard cleat with horns, you can take one turn around the cleat to ease the strain. But always hold the sheet in your hand so that you can let the sail off at a moment's notice.

"After the boat has heeled over to a certain point," Beth continued, "it gets very steady, and it's hard to tip over any farther. That's because the sail is slanted away from the wind, which is forced to spill over the upper leech. To put it another way, the sail deflects the wind so that it doesn't get the full force. At the same time, the windward deck is rising high in the air, and keeps some of the wind off the lower part of the sail, which of course helps prevent the boat from tipping further. In spite of all this, though, good sailors shouldn't ever let their boat tip so far that water begins to slosh into the cockpit."

As the storm cloud moved closer and closer, Beth began to feel that she had made a mistake in trying to get back. "Perhaps," she thought, "we should have stayed on Dutch Ship Island until the storm had either passed or blown itself out." She didn't voice her anxiety to Adam, however.

Soon the sky grew dark, and everything seemed bathed in an eerie, greenish light. They were in for a squall. They could almost smell rain.

By this time, they were fairly close to shore, and knowing that the water would not be too deep for them to anchor, Beth figured that the best plan would be to round up, lower the sails, and anchor. After slacking the mainsheet to lessen the danger of capsizing, she went forward to pull out the anchor from under the foredeck.

"Now I'm going to tie on the anchor line with a fisherman's bend," she said after settling down on the high side with the anchor on her lap. "This anchor is a Danforth and it's especially good for a soft mud bottom because of the large area of its blades, which are called *flukes*. Other popular anchors are the yachtsman, which has small flukes and is good for weed-covered bottoms, and the general-purpose plow anchor that's shaped like a farmer's plow. Now I'd better hurry and take this Danforth up to the bow, where I can lower it after we luff up into the wind."

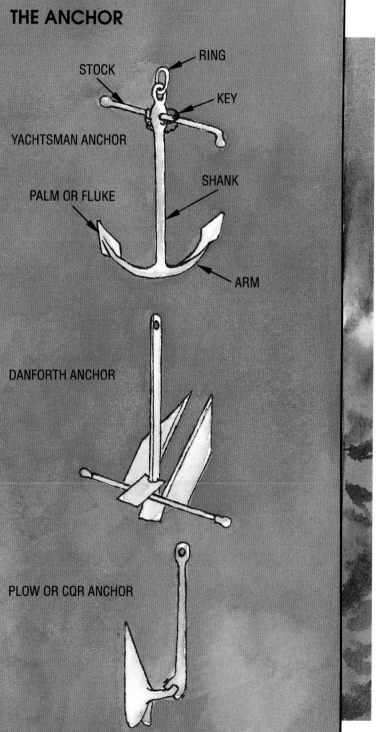

THE ANCHOR

RING

STOCK

KEY

YACHTSMAN ANCHOR

PALM OR FLUKE

SHANK

ARM

DANFORTH ANCHOR

PLOW OR CQR ANCHOR

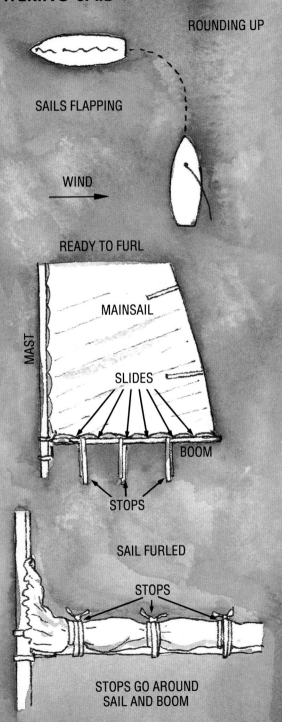

LOWERING SAIL

ROUNDING UP

SAILS FLAPPING

WIND →

READY TO FURL

MAST

MAINSAIL

SLIDES

BOOM

STOPS

SAIL FURLED

STOPS

STOPS GO AROUND
SAIL AND BOOM

Once the anchor was ready, Beth gave careful instructions to Adam about how they would round up and take down the sails. She reached under the foredeck and grabbed a handful of short canvas strips.

"These are called *stops*," she said. "We use them to tie the sails after they're furled. If the boat had slides at the sail's foot, I could thread them through the slot between the mainsail and boom at the proper places. But since our boat doesn't have slides, we have to wait until after the sail is lowered. Then we can throw them twice around the sail and the boom, and tie with a square knot.

"Getting sail off in a breeze can be tricky," warned Beth, "so listen carefully. You stay at the tiller while I go forward and stand by the halyards. Then, when I tell you, round up into the wind slowly until the sails flap. I'll lower the jib and then the mainsail, which you can help furl."

Beth started forward, but as she stepped onto the wet deck, the boat slapped into a choppy wave and gave a sudden lurch. Her foot slipped, she made a wild grab for the shroud—and missed. Cold wetness closed over her.

Since she had a life jacket on, Beth felt no fear of drowning, but she was very concerned about her cousin being alone in the boat.

Adam had a moment of panic when he first saw the mishap, but instinctively he reached for a cockpit cushion and threw it into the water near Beth.

Many thoughts raced through Adam's mind. "I must be calm—must act quickly—must remember what Beth told me. I should jibe so I'll be quick—hmmm—always push the tiller in the opposite direction from the one you want to go!"

Keeping his gaze on Beth, Adam quickly shoved the tiller up to windward and ducked his head low. The boom slammed across, and the boat spun around. Adam felt a little dizzy and confused. He had lost sight of Beth! No, there she was! Her head was bobbing just a little way to windward.

Adam quickly slacked the sheets and rounded up. As the boat slowed down, Beth reached up from the water and grabbed the rail.

"I'm OK," she sputtered, swinging her leg over the side. "Just keep the boat headed into the wind." Adam grabbed Beth by the arm and helped her scramble over the side into the cockpit.

"Way to go!" exclaimed Beth, breathing hard. "You did exactly the right thing. I'm proud of you! We had better hurry, though, and get the sails down. The squall is practically on top of us now."

Beth hurried forward to uncleat the halyards and lower the sails. This time she was very careful. When the sails came down, they made sharp, snapping sounds as the wind whipped them around. Adam could hardly hold onto the mainsail. It was like a wild animal trying to escape capture. Finally he subdued it and firmly secured it with the stops.

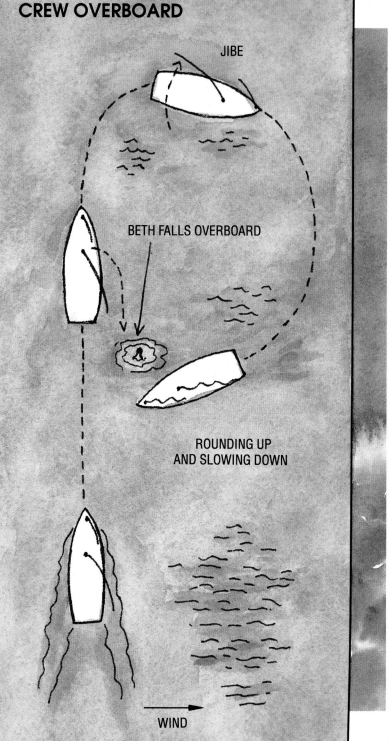

CREW OVERBOARD

JIBE

BETH FALLS OVERBOARD

ROUNDING UP
AND SLOWING DOWN

WIND

31

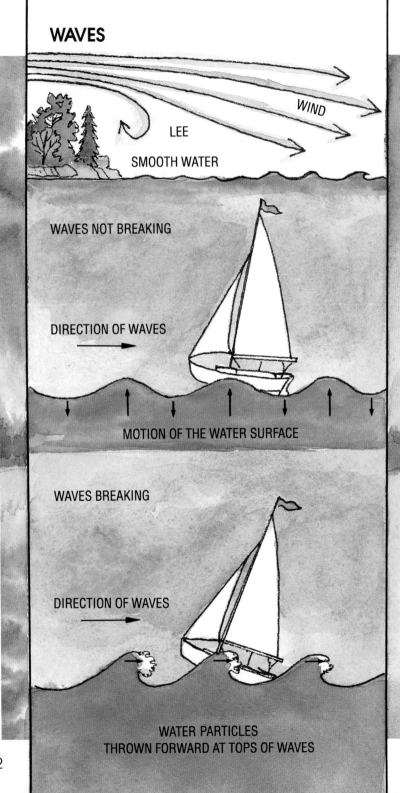

WAVES

WIND

LEE

SMOOTH WATER

WAVES NOT BREAKING

DIRECTION OF WAVES

MOTION OF THE WATER SURFACE

WAVES BREAKING

DIRECTION OF WAVES

WATER PARTICLES
THROWN FORWARD AT TOPS OF WAVES

Just as soon as the sails were down, Beth lowered the anchor and made fast the anchor line. Then she reached under the foredeck and pulled out a large folded piece of canvas.

"This is the *cockpit cover*," she explained. "It goes over the boom and is fastened down on either side of the deck so that it makes a kind of tent. We'll be under cover when it starts raining."

The waves were steadily increasing in size as the first large, cold drops began to fall. An unpleasant bobbing motion rocked the boat.

"Don't worry," said Beth. "When it starts to rain harder, the water will get smoother. A hard rain will flatten out the waves. Also, we're in a good lee here; the land up to windward of us is partly blocking the wind and will prevent large waves from forming. Of course, the closer you are to a windward shore, the smoother the water is. We're close enough here so that we won't have to worry about breaking waves."

"What are they?" asked Adam.

"*Breaking waves* are the kind that have white foam on the top—sailors call them *whitecaps.* They're the worst kind because the little particles of water they're made of have a forward motion. In ordinary waves, the particles move in a circular direction, so a boat is lifted up over the wave. But a *breaking wave* hits a boat instead of lifting it, and can be quite dangerous."

Just then, a bolt of lightning flashed beneath a bank of dark clouds, and a sheet of rain swept across the water toward them. "Here it comes!" cried Beth.

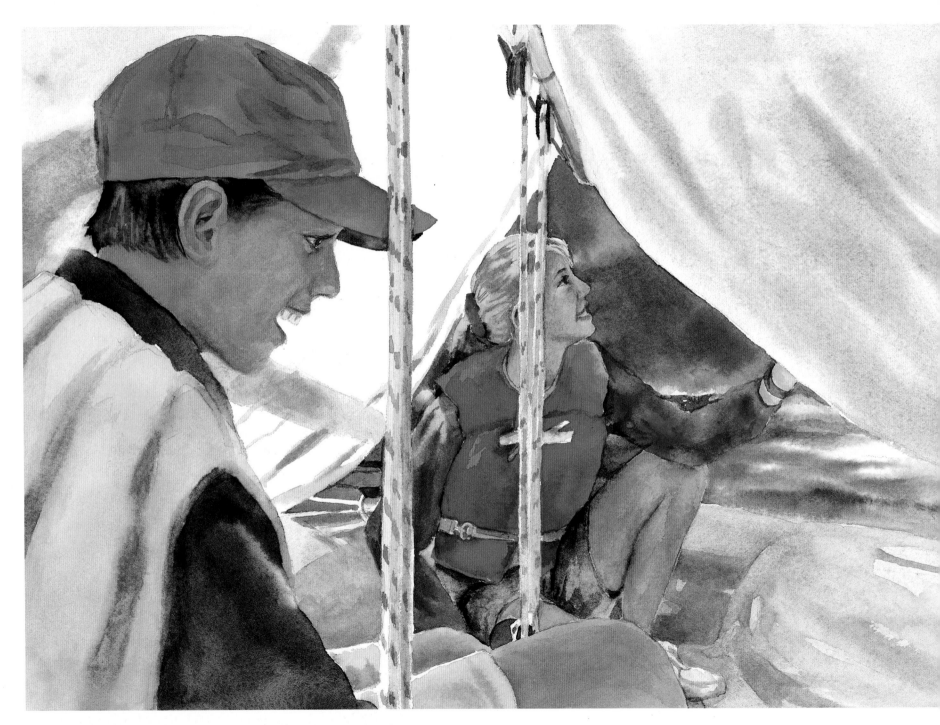

The cousins ducked under the cockpit cover just as the rain hit with a loud splatter. It was dim, but warm and dry, under the canvas shelter. Adam heard many new sounds—the clatter of rain on taut canvas, the hollow pounding of waves against the bow, and the halyards slapping the mast, beating a wild accompaniment to the moans of the wind.

Beth was busily peering out from under the aft end of the cover.

"What are you doing?" asked Adam.

"I'm taking a line of position to see if we're dragging," Beth replied. "I'm lining up that large pine tree on shore with the buoy between the tree and us. I'll check them again in a little while and if they don't line up anymore, and the wind hasn't shifted, it will mean that we've moved."

"Suppose we are moving?" asked Adam anxiously.

"Well, that would mean that the anchor is dragging, and I'd have to let out more scope or anchor line, so the anchor would sink deeper into the bottom and hold better."

Beth's check five minutes later showed that the anchor was holding. It wasn't long before the wind began to subside.

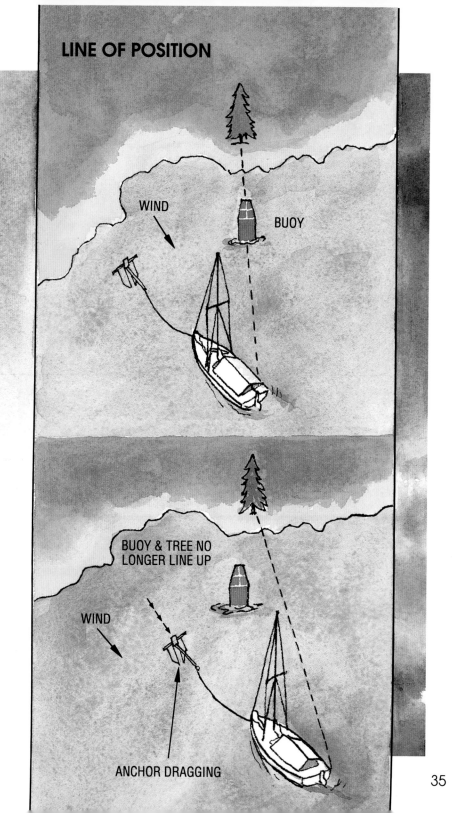

LINE OF POSITION

WIND

BUOY

BUOY & TREE NO LONGER LINE UP

WIND

ANCHOR DRAGGING

35

COILING A LINE

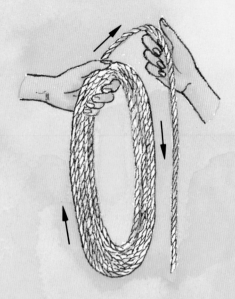

GETTING UNDERWAY FROM ANCHOR

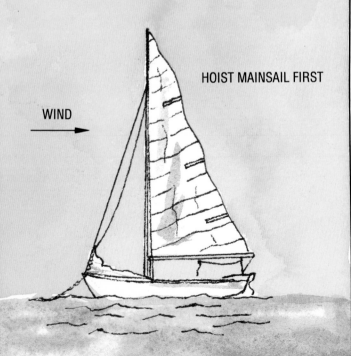

WIND

HOIST MAINSAIL FIRST

"Well, I guess the worst of it is over," said Beth. "You know, sailors have a rhyme that goes

When the rain's before the wind,
You'd better get your topsails in.
When the wind's before the rain,
Shake 'em out and go again.

"We got the wind first, so it's pretty safe to say we won't get any more."

Soon, even the rain stopped. A beam of sunlight broke through the dark clouds and made the water glitter like tinsel.

Beth and Adam crept out from under the canvas, stretched their cramped legs, and slowly began to take down the cover.

"We'll have to get *Gull's Wing* shipshape now," said Beth, looking around at the mess. "A boat should be kept neat so that it'll look good and be easy to handle. We'll have to bail it out and coil all the lines."

When the cover was stowed, Beth showed Adam how to coil a line. She held it in her left hand and made great loops with her right hand in a clockwise direction.

"Coiling is important," she explained, "not only for appearance but for safety. A line will get all tangled up if it's not coiled properly."

At last they were ready to hoist the sails. Beth hoisted the mainsail first, so that the boat would remain headed into the wind with a minimum of swinging around on the anchor line. Then, up went the jib and in came the anchor.

Once again the sloop was under way and heading for home. The sun was shining brightly, and Adam enjoyed its warmth on his back. The boat danced merrily over waves reflecting the intense blue of the clear sky.

"This is far out!" exclaimed Adam. "I've had a super day! I think I've learned a lot about sailing too. You know, Dad said he might give me a little boat of my own next summer if I learned to swim and sail well enough this year."

"All right!" Beth smiled. "There are some very good classes of boats for beginners. Boats like the Optimist pram, Penguin dinghy, and Dyer dhow only have one sail and are easy to handle. Then there are other cat-rigged boats that are a little sportier, like the Butterfly scow, Laser, and Holder Hawk."

"Hey, I'd love to have one of those!" Adam exclaimed.

"I'll bet your dad *will* get you one next year," said Beth. "Especially when I tell him how you rescued me. He'll be proud of you."

Gull's Wing entered the calm waters of the harbor. The two cousins sat quietly, listening to the gurgling sound under the bow and taking in the beauty of the afternoon. Adam realized that his first sail was almost over. It had been an exciting day, and he hated to see it end. Still, it was only a first sail and a whole wonderful summer lay ahead.

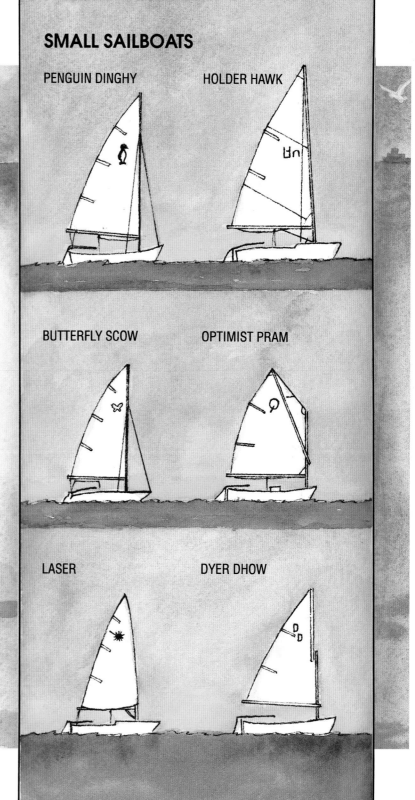

SMALL SAILBOATS

PENGUIN DINGHY

HOLDER HAWK

BUTTERFLY SCOW

OPTIMIST PRAM

LASER

DYER DHOW

QUESTIONS

1. What do sailors call the front of a boat?

2. What is the cockpit on a boat?

3. What line pulls up a sail?

4. What do you call the corner of the sail that is next to the mast and boom?

5. What is a centerboard?

6. What are three ways of finding out which way the wind is blowing?

7. What are the three points of sailing?

8. On entering a harbor, you keep a red buoy on which side?

9. How does a jibe differ from a tack?

10. What buoy is shaped like a cylinder?

11. What are four important pieces of safety equipment for a small boat?

12. What is the starboard tack?

13. Name three knots useful to sailors.

14. How does a yawl differ from a schooner?

15. What is a thunderhead?

16. Should you cleat your mainsheet when sailing in a strong breeze?

17. What are the flukes of an anchor?

18. If a person falls overboard when you are sailing, should you jibe or tack to pick him or her up?

19. What is a lee?

20. Which buoy is red with a pointed top?

21. How do you take a line of position?

22. When a sailor beats a Penguin, is he hitting an Antarctic bird?

1. The bow.

2. The open place in the deck where you sit.

3. A halyard.

4. The tack.

5. A movable board that slides up or down through a narrow box in the center of a boat.

6. By watching your wind indicator, by licking your finger and holding it up to the breeze, and by watching the way wind ripples are being blown across the water's surface.

7. Beating, reaching, and running.

8. On your starboard side (red, right, returning).

9. A tack is a turn into the wind; the sail flaps as it comes across. A jibe is a turn with the wind aft, causing the sail to swing suddenly across the boat.

10. A can is a green buoy shaped like a cylinder.

11. Life preservers, an anchor and line, a bucket or bailer, and a paddle.

12. You are on the starboard tack when your boom is on the port or left side.

13. Bowline, square knot, and clove hitch.

14. A yawl's big mast is forward of its small mast, while a schooner's big mast is abaft (aft of) its small mast.

15. A storm cloud.

16. Not unless it's a jam cleat.

17. The blades that dig into the bottom.

18. A jibe is faster and more direct, but a tack is safer in heavy winds.

19. A shelter or protection from the wind.

20. A red buoy with a pointed top is a nun.

21. One way of obtaining a line of position (on which your boat is located) is by lining up two stationary objects.

22. No, he is sailing a certain type of small boat to windward.